Oscar's House of Smoothies

By Marcy Kelman
Illustrated by Alan Batson
Based on the episode by Fred Stoller

DISNEY PRESS

NEW YORK

𝒟𝒾𝓈𝓃ℯ𝓎 PRESS

Copyright © 2008 by Disney Enterprises, Inc. All rights reserved. Published by Disney Press, an imprint of Disney Book Group. No part of this book may be reproduced or transmitted in any form or by any means, electronic or mechanical, including photocopying, recording, or by any information storage and retrieval system, without written permission from the publisher. For information address Disney Press, 114 Fifth Avenue, New York, New York 10011-5690.

First Edition 10 9 8 7 6 5 4 3 2 1
Library of Congress Cataloging-in-Publication Data on file
ISBN 978-1-4231-1448-2

Manufactured in the USA
For more Disney Press fun, visit www.disneybooks.com

"There, that should do it," Manny said as he finished up his project.
"What are you working on, Manny?" asked Rusty.
"It's a xylophone," Manny answered.

BRRRNG!

"Oh, Manny—I think your xylophone is ringing!" shouted Pat.
Manny chuckled. "No, it's not that kind of phone, Pat. A xylophone is a musical instrument. That's the telephone you hear ringing."

Manny ran to answer the telephone. "Hello, Handy Manny's Repair Shop. You break it, we fix it!"

"Manny? It's Oscar from Oscar's House of 18 Smoothies."

"*Hola*, Oscar! Are you getting ready for your big grand opening today?" inquired Manny.

Oscar sounded a bit panicked. "Well, that's why I'm calling. I accidentally dropped a blender this morning, and it cracked my counter!"

"Gosh, Oscar, I'm sorry that happened," Manny said. "You definitely need that counter to serve smoothies to your customers."

"I know, and the grand opening is in just a few hours!" Oscar cried. "Do you think you can help fix it in time?"

"*No problemo*, Oscar," Manny assured him. "We'll be right over!"

Oscar was relieved. "Thanks so much, Manny!"

On his way to Oscar's store, Manny saw Mr. Lopart sitting in an office chair in front of his candy shop. "*Hola*, Mister Lopart! Wow, is that a new chair?"

"It certainly is," beamed Mr. Lopart. "I thought I'd get a nice new leather chair for when I work behind my desk. See how big and roomy it is?"

"*Sí*, it looks *muy cómoda*—very comfortable," noted Manny. "But it is quite big. Do you need some help bringing it into your store?"

Mr. Lopart laughed. "Aw, no thanks, Manny. This baby's on wheels! It doesn't need to be lifted. I can just wheel it into the shop by myself."

Just then, Fluffy jumped onto Mr. Lopart's lap, causing the office
chair to zip down the sidewalk.

"Mr. Lopart, can I—" started Manny.

"Uh, don't worry, Manny, everything's under *controoooooooool*—"
howled Mr. Lopart, as he quickly whizzed down the sidewalk and
rolled around the corner out of sight.

"Now that's something you don't see in the neighborhood too
often—squeals on wheels!" snickered Turner.

Oscar was relieved to see Manny and the tools arrive at his store. "Welcome to my House of 18 Smoothies. Thanks for coming to help so quickly."

"*De nada*, Oscar. You're welcome," Manny said as he inspected the damaged counter. "This should be an easy fix. I think we'll just need some wood, a couple of hinges, and a few new screws from Kelly's."

"Terrific!" said Oscar. "But before you go, let me show you the very first smoothie I made today. It's my favorite flavor—banana."

"Ooh, I love banana milk shakes!" shouted Pat.

Oscar chuckled. "No, a smoothie is not a milk shake. It looks like a milk shake and even tastes like one, but it is much healthier. The recipes are completely different."

"What's in it?" asked Rusty.

"My smoothies are made with fresh fruit, a little juice, some honey, and ice cubes," explained Oscar.

Look at the ingredients on each recipe card. Which one is Oscar's smoothie recipe? Which one is a milk shake recipe?

Oscar showed Manny and the tools how to make a strawberry smoothie. "Once all the ingredients are in the blender, I simply press the button, and it becomes a thick, delicious smoothie," Oscar said as he poured a glass for Manny.

Manny loved his smoothie. "Mmmm, *delicioso y saludable*! It's delicious and healthy!"

Oscar beamed with pride, pointing to the sign above his counter. "And I don't just have two smoothie flavors. I have eighteen different fruit smoothies customers can choose from!"

Stretch looked up at the sign. After a quick calculation, he realized that there was a problem.

"Um, excuse me, Oscar. But I'm afraid that you made a mistake. I think you need to double-check the number of smoothie flavors you have on your sign."

Can you help Oscar? Count how many smoothie flavors appear on his sign.

"Only seventeen flavors?! What am I going to do?" shrieked Oscar. "All my signs, my cups, and T-shirts say that I have eighteen smoothie flavors!"

Manny tried to calm him down. "*Es fácil*—it's easy, Oscar. All you have to do is come up with another delicious smoothie."

"But I came up with all the smoothie flavors I could possibly think of," sighed Oscar. "What am I going to do now?"

Dusty chimed in. "We can help you come up with another flavor."

"*Sí*, we can dream up something *delicioso* together," Felipe said. "And we'll name it something catchy, like Felipe's Fruity Fireworks! Ooh, or maybe Felipe's Fig-Flavored Frosty—that has a nice ring to it."

"Ick, that idea leaves a bad taste in my mouth," Turner said with a sneer.

"I have a plan," said Manny. "I'll go to Kelly's to buy the supplies we need to fix the counter. While I'm gone, you guys can help Oscar come up with another flavor."

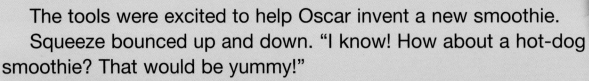

The tools were excited to help Oscar invent a new smoothie.

Squeeze bounced up and down. "I know! How about a hot-dog smoothie? That would be yummy!"

"What about a chicken-noodle-soup smoothie?" suggested Rusty. "That's good for you and tastes great!"

"You know what's good for you?" added Pat. "Toothpaste!"

Oscar started laughing. "A toothpaste smoothie?!"

"Well, you could drink it and brush your teeth with it at the same time," reasoned Pat.

Turner had an idea. "Guys, it would be smart to check out Oscar's kitchen. Let's look around and see if there's an ingredient he hasn't yet used in one of his smoothies."

"Great plan, Turner!" agreed Oscar.

"Okay, here is the menu showing the seventeen smoothies we have available so far," explained Oscar. "If we can just match up the main ingredients on this menu with the items we have here in the kitchen, then we can figure out which ingredient hasn't yet been used in a smoothie."

"Got it," said Stretch. "So, for example, the first smoothie pictured is an apple smoothie."

"And I see apples over there on the kitchen workstation," said Dusty.

"Exactly!" said Oscar.

Look at the menu. Can you name the remaining sixteen smoothies and find their main ingredients on the kitchen counter? Which smoothie ingredient is a vegetable?

Now that you've named all the smoothie ingredients, can you find one item on the counter that hasn't yet been featured in a smoothie?

"It's peanut butter!" shouted Felipe. "That's the ingredient you haven't used yet!"

Just then, Mr. Lopart—still zooming around in his office chair—burst into Oscar's kitchen.

"*Whooooooooooooooooa!*" screamed Mr. Lopart as he crashed into Oscar's kitchen workstation.

Manny returned from Kelly's Hardware Store to find Mr. Lopart and Fluffy on the floor of Oscar's kitchen, covered in food.

"Are you okay?" Manny asked Mr. Lopart as he helped him to his feet.

Mr. Lopart was feeling a bit embarrassed. "Uh, oh, I'm fine, Manny. This worked out perfectly. I wanted to stop by Oscar's smoothie shop anyway to see if it was open yet."

"Actually, we're not ready to open just yet," said Oscar.

"We have to come up with the eighteenth smoothie first," explained Felipe. "And clean up!"

"And fix the counter," Manny reminded everyone.

Mr. Lopart started to wipe some of the food from his face. "Hmm, this looks interesting," Mr. Lopart said, licking his fingers. "Say, it's quite tasty! Is that peanut butter and banana mixed together?"

"Wait a minute!" shouted Turner.

Stretch was excited. "Turner, are you thinking what I'm thinking?"

"That Mr. Lopart is either completely bananas or just a total nut?" grumbled Turner.

"No…that peanut butter and banana could be a new smoothie flavor!" Stretch said.

Oscar grinned. "That is a wonderful idea. I never thought of such an unusual combination!"

"Well, glad we were able to stop by and 'mix it up' with you all," Mr. Lopart snorted. "Come on, Fluffy. We better get back home and get cleaned up for the grand opening. Wouldn't want to miss it!"

After Oscar cleaned up the kitchen, he worked on his new smoothie while Manny and the tools repaired the front counter. Oscar had to find just the right combination of ingredients before the grand opening.

"Okay, we'll put in a little peanut butter, some banana, juice, a dash of cinnamon, some honey, and plenty of crushed ice," Oscar said before flipping the switch on the blender.

Once blended, Oscar tasted his new concoction.

Dusty was anxious. "Well, what do you think? Do you like it?! Do you?!"

"Ahhhh! I love it," gushed Oscar. "I'll call it the Peanut Butter–Banana Smoothie!"

"But…but that's so ordinary, so predictable," said Felipe. "Don't you want some razzle-dazzle in your smoothie name? How about Fantastic Felipe's Nutty Banana Blend? After all, the smoothie is a lovely shade of yellow, just like me, and…"

"Okay, I take back what I said about Mr. Lopart," Turner interrupted. "You're the one who's totally nutty and completely bananas!"

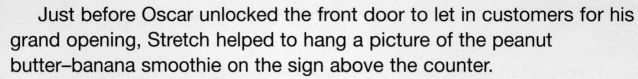

Just before Oscar unlocked the front door to let in customers for his grand opening, Stretch helped to hang a picture of the peanut butter–banana smoothie on the sign above the counter.

"My eighteenth smoothie—I couldn't have thought of it without your help, tools! And, of course, without the help of Mr. Lopart's runaway chair," laughed Oscar.

Squeeze giggled. "It's true. We couldn't have created the perfect smoothie without Mr. Lopart's not-so-smooth moves!"

Manny smiled. "Well, it could have been a recipe for disaster, but luckily we had the main ingredient needed to do the job right—teamwork!"